Impartial Relation of the Military Operations Which Took Place in Ireland

IMPARTIAL RELATION

OF THE

MILITARY OPERATIONS

WHICH TOOK PLACE IN

IRELAND,

IN CONSEQUENCE OF THE LANDING OF A BODY OF

FRENCH TROOPS,

Under General Humbert, in August, 1798.

BY AN OFFICER,
Who served in the Corps, under the Command of His Excellency
MARQUIS CORNWALLIS.

LONDON:

PRINTED FOR T. EGERTON, AT THE MILITARY
LIBRARY, NEAR WHITEHALL.

MDCCXCIX.

1799.

IMPARTIAL RELATION, &c.

HAVING obferved that the meafures purfued by Lord Cornwallis, during the attempt made by the fmall body of French troops, which landed in in Ireland under General Humbert in Auguft laft, as well as the operations of the King's troops, have been in general mifunderftood, and above all, that very grofs mifreprefentations have been made of the means which were employed to defeat the enemy's object, I am induced to lay before the public, a fhort ftatement of facts, which, as an officer employed at that period in Ireland, I can, from perfonal obfervation, bring forward as authentic; and to which I have been enabled to give a greater degree of correctnefs, from having been fo fortunate as to procure, from the communication of official documents, much information, of which I could not otherwife have been in poffeffion.

B

It

It may be neceſſary to make a few previous ob-ſervations, on the ſtate of defence the country was in at the time General Humbert landed at Killala.

Before Marquis Cornwallis arrived in Ireland, the ſyſtem which had been purſued for the ſuppreſ-ſion of rebellion (which for a conſiderable time had ſpread without aſſuming a decided and collec-tive form) added to the deſire of affording pro-tection to individual property, had neceſſarily oc-caſioned a very great diſperſion of the troops: hence conſiderable difficulties aroſe, when circum-ſtances of a more ſerious nature required the af-ſembling any where, a body of troops calculated to oppoſe decidedly the attempts of an enemy, who had collected in ſufficient force to become as formidable to the general intereſts and ſecurity of the kingdom, as he had for ſome time proved to thoſe of individuals; and of this, the time which elapſed before Lieutenant General Lake could collect a corps that was thought equal to the at-tack of the rebels at Vinegar Hill, and in other parts of the county of Wexford, appears a ſuffi-cient proof.

Much as the Lord Lieutenant could have wiſhed immediately to make ſuch a diſpoſition of the troops, as ſhould more effectually provide for the general defence of the kingdom againſt foreign at-tempts,

tempts, or for its security against any serious internal commotions, it was impossible, without much caution, and, from many considerations, without much delay, to carry into execution any arrangement for collecting, in the first instance the detachments of regiments which were most dispersed, and in the next for assembling and stationing, at particular points, corps which might be moved as circumstances should require, and might act with expedition and effect; independent of which, the state of disturbance in which the counties of Wexford, Wicklow, Kilkenny, Kildare, and parts of Dublin still continued, required a very large proportion of the force, and this consideration naturally encreased the difficulty of forming and executing any arrangement, having a general object in view.

These difficulties had however been in great measure overcome, the arrangement was made and on the point of execution, when a report was received in Dublin, from Major General Hutchinson, of the landing of the enemy, on the 22d of August, in Killala Bay, on the western coast of Ireland, in which quarter of the kingdom the troops were at that time very thinly scattered; the province of Connaught having continued in a state of comparative quiet when rebellion was raging in other parts of Ireland.

The

The French landed near Killala, about fix in the evening, from three frigates and a brig, to the number of 1260 rank and file, with a very confiderable proportion of officers, and three pieces of cannon. A fmall party of the Leicefter Fencible Infantry, under Lieutenant Sills of that regiment, and the yeomanry of the town of Killala, attempted to oppofe their progrefs to the town, but were furrounded and taken prifoners, having three men killed. The Bifhop of Killala, Dean Thompfon, and fome other clergymen, were alfo made prifoners by the French, who, upon entering the town, diftributed handbills to the populace, declaring themfelves friends of the people, and their deliverers from oppreffion.*

Upon receiving information of thefe events, the Tyrawley Yeoman Cavalry affembled in Ballina, where they were joined on the morning of the 23d by fome volunteers, and before night by feveral troops of yeoman cavalry, and a detachment of the carabineers, under Major Keir, who took the command in Ballina.—On the morning of the 24th, the French marched from Killala towards Ballina, but meeting with greater oppofition than they probably expected, they retreated to Killala. In the evening, Major Keir having been reinforced by feveral

See Appendix, Note 1. p. 45.

corps

corps of yeomanry, advanced to within one mile and a half of Killala, but was obliged again to fall back, after an unfuccefsful fkirmifh, in which the Rev. Mr. Fortefcue, rector of Ballina, and two men of the carabineers, were wounded, the former mortally. In the retreat, Major Keir met Colonel Sir Thomas Chapman, who was advancing with three troops of the carabineers, and fome infantry.—Sir Thomas Chapman having collected the troops, took poft on an eminence near Moyne Abbey, whence he retreated, unmolefted, at 12 o'clock at night, through Ballina to Foxford.

During all this time, the French had not been joined by any confiderable number of the inhabitants of the county of Mayo; who indeed, except in the immediate neighbourhood of Killala, remained perfectly quiet; nor did they appear more difpofed to rife in the other parts of the province of Connaught. The numbers of the French had been much exaggerated, few reports making them amount to lefs than 1800 men, with 12 or 15 pieces of cannon.—The frigates failed from Killala Bay on the 24th. Brigadier General Taylor had on that day marched from Sligo, with about 250 men of the Leicefter Fencibles, and about the fame number of yeomanry, towards Ballina; but finding that the place had been occupied by the French

B 3

upon

upon the retreat of the King's troops, he returned to Sligo,

Major General Hutchinson, who commanded in the province of Connaught, and who, with Major General French, was in the town of Galway, upon the first intelligence of the enemy's landing, had moved the Longford regiment of militia upon Gort, and upon receiving further accounts, determined upon ordering all the troops he could collect, to march towards the counties of Mayo and Sligo, which, however, from the slender force under his command, could not be done without leaving the counties of Leitrim and Roscommon open, and the bridges on the upper Shannon almost without protection. The troops with which he moved towards Castlebar, were the Kerry Militia, from Galway; a detachment of the Fraser Fencibles, from Tuam; the Kilkenny Militia, from Loughrea; the Longford, from Gort; a detachment of Lord Roden's Fencible Dragoons, and four six-pounders and a howitzer, from Athenry. These troops were afterwards joined by the skeleton of the 6th regiment (about 100 men) from Galway, which town remained garrisoned by a few corps of yeomanry only. The disposition of the country continued favourable, which was not however absolutely the case towards Carrick on Shannon, to

which

which place the city of Limerick regiment of militia were ordered, from Athlone, by Brigadier General Barnett.

In confequence of the circumftances and movements above ftated, reports of which were received in Dublin on the 24th Auguft, Lord Cornwallis immediately ordered Lieutenant General Lake to proceed to Galway, to take the command of the troops affembling in Connaught, meaning in perfon to collect the troops that could be marched from Leinfter, at Athlone or Carrick on Shannon, as circumftances fhould point out.

The following difpofition was made of the march of thofe troops, towards the Shannon, for occupying fixed ftations and fecuring the communications, and with the further view to the prefervation of peace in the difturbed counties of Dublin, Wicklow, Wexford, Meath, Kildare, and Louth.

FORCE

FORCE *to move towards the* SHANNON.

1ſt Light Infantry	With M. General Moore, from Sallins, by Canal to Athlone.
2d ditto ditto	
100th Regiment	
Suffolk Fencibles	From Kilcullen to Athlone.
Downſhire Militia	To colleɕt on Birr to Balli-naſloe.
Armagh	On their march to Birr, to pro-ceed to Ballinaſloe, the other three companies to follow.
Four Companies	
Reay Fencibles	From Kilcock to Longford.
Sutherland Fencibles	From Drogheda and Dundalk to Longford.
Antrim Militia	From Kilcullen to Athlone.
Bucks —	Flank Companies from Dub-lin to Longford.
Warwick —	
Louth Militia —	From Limerick to Galway.
5th Dragoon Guards	From Dublin to Athlone.
2d Foot —	With Major General Hunter from Wexford to Kilkenny, thence to move upon the Shannon.
29th —	

Amounting in the whole to about 7000 men.

REGIMENTS

REGIMENTS *to move to fixed Stations:*

Cork City Militia ⎱ To occupy the Canal, Cel-
Londonderry Militia ⎰ bridge, &c.

Carlow Militia — Drogheda and Dundalk.

Invernefs Fencibles   Trim and Kilcock.

Cork City Militia   Naas.

89th Regiment ⎰ Baltinglafs and Hackets
⎱ Town.

5th Dragoons ⎰ From Loughlins Town to
⎱ Dublin.

7th Dragoon ⎰ To occupy Phillips Town,
Guards ⎱ Birr, &c.

4th Dragoon Guards ⎰ Maryborough, and to keep
⎰ open the communication
⎱ with Limerick.

9th Dragoons ⎰ Carlow and Kilkenny, and
⎰ to keep open the commu-
⎱ nication with Dublin.

Hompefch's Chaffeurs ⎰ Clonmell, to keep open
⎰ the communication to
⎱ Cork.

One Company from Lim-
erick garrifon, to be de-
tached to Nenagh.

Chefhire Fencibles ⎱ Their march from Kilkenny
Glengary Fencibles ⎰ to be fufpended.

Dublin County Militia—From Ferns to Wexford.

Remain

Remain in the Counties of Dublin, Wicklow, Wexford, Meath, Kildare and Louth.

Dublin Garrison	5th Dragoons. Angus Fencibles. Bucks Militia. Warwick Militia. 68th Regiment. Fermanagh Militia.

N. B. The Yeomanry may be called 5000 effective men.

Loughlinftown — Antient Britifh Fencibles.
Wicklow, &c. — King's County Militia.
Arklow — Sligo Militia.
Rathdrum — Leitrim Militia.
Gorey — Durham Fencibles.
Wexford — Dublin County Militia.
Ennifcorthy — South Cork Militia.
Newtown Barry — Cavan ditto.
Rofs — 1 Battalion Foot Guards.
Baltinglafs — 89th Regiment.
Kilcock and Trim — Invernefs Fencibles.
Naas — } Waterford Militia, Dumfries Fencibles, Dublin City Militia.
Kilcullen —
Dundalk and Drogheda } Carlow Militia, Dumfries Fencible Cavalry.
Canal Line to Monaftereven } Cork City Militia, Londonderry Militia.

Arrangement, 24th Auguft, 1798.

Independent

Independent of the above difpofition, Major General Nugent was directed to affemble a corps on the frontier of his diftrict (the Northern) towards Sligo.

Lieutenant Colonel Maxwell, of the 23d Dragoons, who commanded at Ennifkillen, had, on the firft alarm, marched from thence to Sligo, with the whole of his garrifon, confifting of about 500 men, of which, upwards of one-half Yeomanry, and two howitzers and two fix pounders; and the fmall garrifon of Ballyfhannon had alfo marched to Sligo. Brigadier General Champagné, upon his arrival at Ennifkillen, from Armagh, fent orders to Major Packenham, quartered at Granard, with two troops of the 23d Dragoons, to proceed to Carrick on Shannon, and collected at Ennifkillen, a garrifon of about 600 Yeoman Cavalry and Infantry. He further directed a garrifon of Yeomanry to be ftationed at Ballyfhannon, and the Yeomanry of the baronies of his diftrict, bordering on the fea, to collect at Donegall. Lord Portarlington, who commanded the Queen's County regiment, at Strabane and Armagh, was alfo to affemble the yeoman corps in his neighbourhood, fo as to enable him to fend either to Ennifkillen or Ballyfhannon, a reinforcement of 600 men.

Major

Major General Nugent had ordered Colonel Lord William Bentinck from Armagh, to proceed with the proportion of the Breadalbane Fencibles, quartered there and at Monaghan, as well as a part of the 24th Dragoons, to Ennifkillen. The 3d light battalion to proceed from Blaris Hutts to Lurgan, and the North Lowland Fencibles from Dungannon to Augher and Clogher, there to remain. The whole of the Yeomanry corps in the Northern Diſtrict were ordered to hold themfelves in readinefs to take the field ; but, unlefs abfolutely neceffary, it was not thought expedient to remove them from agricultural and other occupations, which required their immediate attention.

Major General Hutchinfon arrived at Caſtlebar on the 25th, he found the country through which he paffed, as well as the neighbourhood of that place, in a ſtate of perfect tranquility. It however, was reported, that the French who remained at Killala and Ballina had been joined by 1800 men ; and Major General Hutchinfon having very foon reafon to think, that notwithſtanding the firſt appearance of things, the inhabitants began to favour the enemy's project, and were rifing in confiderable numbers, he was induced to give up the plan he had at firſt formed of attacking them, and judged it advifeable to write to Lord Cornwallis for further affiftance. Brigadier General Taylor moved from

Sligo

Sligo towards Caftlebar, on the 25th, with about 1200 men, chiefly Yeomanry.

Lord Cornwallis arrived at Phillipftown on the 26th with the 100th Regiment, the 1ft and 2d battalions of light infantry, and the flank companies of the Bucks and Warwick Militia, and on the 27th proceeded to Kilbeggan, the troops having made a progrefs of forty four Irifh miles (about fixty Englifh) in two days.

In the mean time reports were received from Lieutenant General Dundas, who commanded in the county of Kildare, that there were grounds to apprehend that a general infurrection was intended in that county, that notices had been circulated by the difaffected, calling upon the people to rife, and that many of the inhabitants had abandoned their habitations; in confequence of which, he had been under the neceffity of detaining part of the reinforcements ordered to Connaught.

Very early in the morning of the 28th, Major Hardy, Affiftant Quarter Mafter General, arrived at Kilbeggan, with a report from Lieutenant General Lake, of the refult of an attack made by the French, on the morning of the 27th, on Major General Hutchinfon's corps at Caftlebar, which Lieutenant General Lake had joined the night before.

before. Upon receiving intelligence that the enemy were advancing towards Caftlebar, the troops were ordered to occupy a pofition in front, which covered that town, as well as the greater part of the county of Mayo, and was well calculated for keeping up the communication with Brigadier General Taylor, who had advanced to Foxford, and whofe corps had been reinforced by the Kerry Militia and the Leicefter Fencibles, which had been detached from Caftlebar. The enemy's attack was made about feven in the morning.

The French, with about 1500 rebels, advanced in regular order upon the King's troops, who waited their approach in the pofition they occupied. The artillery, under Captain Shortall, was admirably ferved and made a vifible impreffion, infomuch that the enemy's advance was actually checked, and they began to difperfe ; at this critical moment our troops, as if feized with a fudden panic and without any apparent reafon, gave way; and notwithftanding every effort made by Lieutenant General Lake, Major Generals Hutchinfon and Trench, and the very meritorious exertions of all their officers, they could not be rallied, but retired in confufion through Caftlebar towards Hollymount. Lord Roden's Fencible Dragoons, however, fhewed great gallantry upon this as they had upon all other occafions ; they protected the retreat

of

of the infantry and even recovered a six-pounder which the French had pushed forward through Castlebar. The skeleton of the Sixth Regiment, under Major Macbean also behaved with spirit in the action.

The following is the return of killed, wounded, and missing, and of guns lost upon this unfortunate occasion. Of the soldiers of the Longford and Kilkenny Militia returned missing, the greater part had deserted to the enemy. The loss of the French in killed and wounded (and resulting almost entirely from the effect of the artillery) was afterwards found to have been far more considerable than that of the King's Troops.

Return

Return of Killed, Wounded, and Missing, of the Troops under the command of Lieutenant General LAKE. Castlebar, 27th August, 1798.

	Killed		Wounded			Missing								Horses		
	Serjeants	Rank and File	Lieutenants	Serjeants	Rank and File	Majors	Captains	Lieutenants	Ensigns	Staff	Serjeants	Drummers	Rank and File	Killed	Wounded	Missing
Light Brigade Irish Artillery		2			2								12	6		32
Carabineers																
6th Foot		11		2	2	1	1	1	2	1	1		25			
Frafer Fencibles		23			9			1			1	1	16			
Royal Longford Militia	1	12	2	1	10	1	2	1	1	1	8	1	146			
Kilkenny Militia		4			6			3					42			
Galway Volunteers													10			
	1	52	2	3	29	2	3	6	3	2	10	2	2,251	6		32

No return of the Carabineers was received.

Names

NAMES OF PRISONERS.

6th Foot.

Major Macbean
Enfign Hill
Enfign Martelli, miffing
Enfign Burrows, do.
Affiftant Surgeon Walters, do.
Lieutenant M'Quire, killed.

Royal Longford Militia.

Captain Chambers, wounded
Lieutenant and Affiftant Surgeon, wounded and
miffing.
Enfign Sedwith, wounded
Lieutenant and Adjutant Telford, prifoner.

Kilkenny Regiment of Militia.

Major Alcock, wounded and prifoner
Lieutenant and Adjutant Walford, wounded do.
One battalion gun loft, with tumbril, &c. &c.

Galway Volunteers.

2 Captains and 3 Lieutenants, miffing
2 Lieutenants, wounded
1 Lieutenant, prifoner, but refcued
Volunteer French, wounded and miffing.

C   Frafer

Frafer Fencibles.

Loft, two battalion guns
Ammunition, Tumbrils, &c. &c.

Ordnance, Royal Artillery.

Curricle guns and carts, four	4
Battalion guns, five	5
Total	9

Longford Militia.

Loft, two battalion guns
Ammunition, &c.

* Immediately after receiving the report of this affair, Lord Cornwallis proceeded to Athlone, where, upon his arrival, he received information from different quarters, but particularly from Mr. O'Donnell, Captain of the Newport Pratt Yeomanry, and from a Lieutenant of the Carabineers, both of whom had left Tuam in the morning that Lieutenant General Lake had retired to that place, and had been followed by the French who were ftated to have driven his corps out of the town, and to have taken poffeffion of it. However extraordinary fuch an event appeared, the information was fo pofitive and fo circumftantial, that there feemed

---

* Notes 2 and 3, with tranflations.

no grounds for doubting its authenticity, although it afterwards proved to be perfectly unfounded.

The French were further said to have been joined by very confiderable numbers of the inhabitants, and to have diftributed arms to them; and Sir Thomas Chapman who had retired to French Park, alfo reported that the country to the Northward, towards Sligo, was in open rebellion. Every poffible precaution became indifpenfable. His Excellency therefore determined, at all events, to halt at Athlone, until joined by the Sutherland and Reay Fencibles, who were directed to haften their march from Longford, and to wait the arrival of the Queen's and 29th Regiment, then on their march from Kilkenny, and who were expected to join in the courfe of five days. The brigade of Guards from Waterford, Rofs, and Clonmell had alfo been directed to move towards the Shannon, and the Yeomanry, throughout the kingdom, were ordered upon permanent duty. The city of Limerick Regiment was ordered from Carrick on Shannon to Ennifkillen.

Every precaution was taken to fecure the town of Athlone againft attack, and piquets and patroles were far advanced on the roads to Ballinafloe and Tuam.

The

The firſt diviſion of the Sutherland and Reay Fencibles arrived at Athlone late on the 28th, the remainder on the 29th. Letters were on that day received from Lieutenant General Lake, ſtating that he had been under the neceſſity of continuing his retreat to Tuam; during which he had been joined near Hollymount, by the Louth Militia. A flag of truce had arrived on the 29th at Tuam, with 12 of the officers taken priſoners at Caſtlebar, from whom he learnt that numbers of the inhabitants had joined the French, as well as many deſerters from the Longford and Kilkenny regiments. The French remained at Caſtlebar, having a few piquets in front of the town; Ballinrobe, Hollymount, Swineford, &c. were occupied by the rebels. Lieutenant General Lake added, that from the reduction which had taken place in his corps, and the want of artillery and ammunition, he ſhould be obliged to draw nearer to Athlone.

Upon the receipt of the above report, Lord Cornwallis determined to move forward on the 30th with the corps under his command. Orders were ſent to Lieutenant General Lake to halt the Sixth Regiment, the Louth Militia, and the detachment of the Fraſer Fencibles, and Lord Roden's Fencible Dragoons at Ballinamore, and to direct the remainder of his corps (the conduct of which during the retreat had been very diſorderly)

to

to proceed on their march to Athlone. Brigadier General Taylor, who with the troops he had collected, was retreating upon Carrick on Shannon, was ordered to halt at Boyle.

In the mean time reports were received from Captain Thatcher, who with a detachment of the Northumberland Fencibles, was stationed at Kilbeggan, that an attack was intended on his post, by about 1000 Rebels collected in the neighbourhood, who were to be joined by those from the County of Kildare. In consequence, Brigadier General Barnett was directed to order the Yeomanry from Moat and the neighbourhood to Kilbeggan, and if necessary to detach further from the Garrison of Athlone, when enabled so to do by the arrival of the Longford and Kilkenny Regiments.

Major General Nugent reported on the 29th, that he had ordered the 3d Battalion of Light Infantry, from Enniskillen to Sligo. That the Limerick City Regiment had arrived at Enniskillen and remained there with the Breadalbane Fencible Regiment, whilst the Argyll Fencibles occupied Belturbet, and that he had ordered all the boats at Lough Erne, as well as in Lough Neagh and the River Bann, to be secured, to prevent the possibility

C 3

of a junction, should the disaffected in the North attempt a rising.

Lord Cornwallis's corps arrived and encamped on the 30th, near Ballinamore, where his Excellency halted the 31st, to give the Queen's and 29th regiments time to join him. These regiments had made a most expeditious march from Wexford; and arrived at Ballinasloe on the 31st. Lieutenant Colonel Craufurd (Deputy Quartermaster General) was sent forward towards Castlebar, with a strong patrole of Lord Roden's Fencibles, and Hompesch's Dragoons, to ascertain the position and proceedings of the enemy. Brigadier General Taylor was directed to wait further orders at Boyle, to send constant and strong patroles in every direction, and very far in his front. The brigade of Guards was ordered to halt at Birr, where they would be within reach should their support be required.

Brigadier General Barnett reported from Athlone, that the forges both in Roscommon and on the Leinster side, were busily employed in making pikes, and that a great number of trees had been cut down for that purpose.

Lieutenant Colonel Craufurd had, on the 31st, proceeded to Holly Mount, and to Kilmain, near which

which place he took a few rebels prisoners ; and he learnt that a considerable body of armed rebels, commanded by Mr. George Blake, were in possession of Ballinrobe. Not having any infantry with him, and the horses of the cavalry being fatigued, he judged it adviseable not to push any further on that day, and returned to Hollymount.

Lord Cornwallis, on the 1st September, proceeded to Knock Hill, where his corps encamped. His Excellency here received a further report from Colonel Craufurd, who had advanced about five miles from Hollymount, in the direction of Castlebar, without meeting with an enemy. He was informed by persons who had escaped from Castlebar, that the French had been joined by many of the inhabitants of the district, to the North of the line, from Ballinrobe to Clare, but particularly from the Western and most mountainous parts of the county of Mayo ; in which neighbourhood it was said that several gentlemen headed the insurgents.

Colonel Craufurd also sent a patrole into Ballinrobe, where they found about 80 men in arms, whom they dispersed, killing 12, the remainder having with Mr. Blake left the place for Castlebar in the morning. A flag of truce arrived at Hollymount on the same day, under the pretence of

C 4   bringing

bringing in two of the carabineers, but evidently for the purpose of reconnoitring.

Lord Cornwallis on the 2d arrived and encamped about two miles in front of Tuam, where he was joined by the Queen's and 29th regiments, and the annexed was the order of battle of his Excellency's corps on that day.

To those who have been at the trouble of confidering the state of the country, as well as the obvious circumstances which had prepared and produced the enemy's first success at Castlebar, it may be unnecessary to observe on the propriety and the prudence of the motives which probably induced Lord Cornwallis not to place himself in a situation to give or to receive a decisive action, until his corps should be composed of troops in which he could firmly confide. The result of the action of Castlebar was a sufficient proof of what might be expected from a second check, particularly if received by any part of the corps which was then moving forward. Its effect would not have been confined to the increase of men and means, which would have resulted to the small corps of French troops, whose existence rested solely on the degree of support they received; it would have extended to the disaffected in every part of the kingdom, who,

ORDER of ARQUIS CORNWALLIS

bbell

Roxburgh Fenc.D

Sutherland Fenc.

5.ᵗ Dragoon Guards

1 Fen

Hompesh's Drag.

M. Gen.ᵗ Campbell.

M.Gen.ᵗ Hutchinso

M.Gen.ᵗ Hunter.....

M.Gen.ᵗ Moore....

who, there was good reason to believe, had only continued quiet as yet, because they were unwilling to truft to the firft fuccefs of fo fmall a foreign fupport, in an undertaking which, if it ultimately failed, muft affect their lives and properties, and becaufe they were looking forward to the arrival of an additional French force which was known to be prepared in Breft, and which was prevented by our fleet cruizing off that port, from failing at the fame time that General Humbert left Rochfort.

In many parts of the country, however, and particularly in thofe which had been the feat of former difturbance, the difaffected were not influenced by cautious confiderations, but were actually in arms and avowing their purpofe of giving every poffible affiftance to the French, and of impeding, by every means in their power, the operations of the King's troops. Large bodies were collecting in the counties of Kildare, Weftmeath, and Longford; Rofcommon was overawed by the vicinity of the troops alone, and even the capital was threatened with ferious difturbances and rifings, which could not either be faid to have fubfided in the counties of Wicklow, Wexford, and Carlow, although they had been reduced to a ftate of comparative quiet previous to the withdrawing of Major General Moore's corps.

Lord

Lord Cornwallis had received pofitive information that the Breft expedition was deftined for the
North of Ireland, and that it was only waiting a
favourable opportunity to elude the vigilance of our
fleets; General Humbert's remaining at Caftlebar
might with reafon be attributed to the expecta-
tion of receiving reinforcements himfelf, and of a
co-operation from the corps wihch was to fail from
Breft; and as long as he continued ftationary,
there were not any grounds attaching to his corps
folely, which could juftify any meafure on the part
of Lord Cornwallis, not adopted with a moral
certainty of fuccefs, or which was attended with
the moft diftant probability of a trifling check, or
partial rifk.—Thefe obfervations, if admitted as
juft, will fufficiently account for his Excellency's
defire to be joined by fo refpectable a reinforcement as that of two old and well difciplined
regiments of the line, before he proceeded to ftrike
a blow, which in its effects involved confiderations
far more important than the mere operations which,
under other circumftances, would have been
directed againft the enemy with whom he had to
contend.

His Excellency determined to reinforce Brigadier
General Taylor's corps, fo as to enable it to act
with decifion and vigour upon the enemy's left,
and more effectually to fecure the country to the
Eaftward

STATE *of the* B[r]able

ROBERT TAYL[798].

QUARTERS.		d	Men attached to the Battalion Guns.
Boyle	—Royal I[r]	—	—
Col. Chapman	⎰ Carabin[o]	—
	Manorh[4]	—
	Lowther[2]	—
	Newpor[9]	—
Lieut. Colonel Maxwell	⎰ Twenty[3]	—
	Roxburg[8]	—
	1ſt. Ferr[9]	—
	Carberr[5]	—
Lt. Col. Croſbie	Kerry M[—]	30
Lieut. Colonel Bulkeley	⎰ Northan[—]	—
	Enniſkil[—]	—
	Fermana[—]	—
	Liſbello[r]	—
	Beleck [—]	—
	Wattle-[—]	—
	Lurg T[r]	—
Lt. Col. Sparrow	Eſſex F[e]	30
Lieut. Colonel Macartney	⎰ Prince o[—]	30
	Ballymo[—]	—
	Manorh[—]	—
	Caſtleba[—]	—
	Lowther[—]	—
	Sligo In[—]	—
	Weſtpo[r]	—
		o	90

Eaſtward and Northward, ſhould the enemy, inſtead of awaiting his Excellency's attack at Caſtlebar, attempt to puſh either towards Sligo or the Shannon. The annexed return of the force under Brigadier General Taylor, conſiſting in great meaſure of very ſmall corps, and of detachments, will point out to every military man, the neceſſity of rein-forcing it, before it could be brought forward and placed in a ſituation where it might perhaps be under the neceſſity of acting independently.

Lieutenant General Lake therefore marched early on the 3d, with the Reay Fencibles and the Armagh Militia, by Dunmore, to Ballinlough, whence he was to proceed to French Park. General Taylor received orders on the ſame day, to advance with the whole of his corps to French Park, where Lieutenant General Lake would take the com-mand. Brigadier General Taylor's advanced poſts were on the 3d puſhed forward to Ballaghy, Swine-ford, Kilkelly, &c.; and Lieutenant Colonel Crau-furd was ordered to patrole from Hollymount towards Clare, Ball, Balcurra, &c. and to en-deavour to aſcertain the poſition of the enemy. The reports of perſons who had eſcaped from the country in the poſſeſſion of the enemy, ſtated, that they intended if poſſible to make a ſtand at Caſtle-bar, where they had been joined by about 8000 rebels, who were principally armed with pikes;

ſhould

should they however be under the necessity of retreating from Castlebar, that they proposed taking refuge in the mountainous parts of the County of Mayo, and there wait further reinforcements from France.

Major General Nugent proceeded on the 2d. to make the necessary arrangements for the security of Sligo, in case of attack; he had ordered the Limerick City Regiment from Enniskillen, as a reinforcement to its garrison, which was formed of the following corps, Major General Nugent having sent the third battalion of Light Infantry to Brigadier General Taylor's corps, and having received in exchange, the Essex Regiment of Fencible Infantry.

Garrison of Sligo.

	MEN
Essex Fencibles—Lieutenant Colonel Sparrow	250
Limerick City Militia—Colonel Vereker	300
Sligo Yeoman Infantry — —	100
Manor Hamilton Infantry —	55
Ballymote Infantry —	45
Artenan Infantry — —	50
Twenty-Fourth Dragoons—Captain Whistler	36
Drumcliff Yeomanry Cavalry —	20
	856

A baggage Guard of the Prince of Wales's Fencibles.

Artillery

Artillery at Sligo.

2 Medium Six-pounders—returned from Boyle
2 Field Pieces of the Effex Fencibles
2 Curricle Six-pounders, left by the Light Battalion, and now attached to the Limerick Regiment.
With Detachments of the Royal Artillery.

Colonel Vereker, the fenior officer, was ordered not to move out of the town, unlefs he found he could not maintain it, in which cafe he was to retire upon Ballyfhannon. After making the neceffary arrange-ments at Sligo and Ballyfhannon, Major General Nugent returned to Ennifkillen.

On the 4th, Lord Cornwallis moved forward with the whole of his corps, and encamped in the rear of Hollymount: Here he received information that the enemy had entrenched himfelf behind Caftlebar, on the ground where the attack was made on Lieutenant-general Lake's corps, and that he had pofted the rebels in Caftlebar and the vil-lages in its front. His Excellency, upon this in-telligence, determined to march from Hollymount at day-break, with the whole of his corps, with the view of attacking the enemy ; and directed Lieu-tenant-general Lake to advance to Ballaghy, to pufh his advanced pofts to Foxford and Caftlebar, and

and to communicate with him by patroles on the roads from Swiniford to Molina and Ball.

In the evening, however, of the 4th, Lord Cornwallis received information, that the enemy had marched early in the morning from Caftlebar, with the whole of his force, in the direction of Foxford, and a confirmation of this report was received from Lieutenant-Colonel Crauford, who had pufhed into Caftlebar, upon learning that the enemy had left the place, where he found feveral wounded officers and men, about 50 barrels of powder, an ammunition-waggon, and fome arms. The intelligence he received was contradictory, fome reports ftating that the enemy was marching to Sligo, others that he intended an attack on Lieutenant-General Lake's corps, but not being able to gain any pofitive information, he determined to follow the enemy at day-break the next morning, and to hang upon his rear, with the detachment of Hompefch and Lord Roden's fencible dragoons, which formed the corps under his orders. Lieutenant-Colonel Crauford, alfo apprehended in Caftlebar, Mr. John Moore, whom General Humbert had appointed Prefident of the Council, for the Province of Connaught.*

Note 4, and Tranflation.

A3

As it was impossible to form a correct judgment
of General Humbert's object, Lord Cornwallis sent
directions to Lieutenant-General Lake to follow
him, and to harrass and impede his march, but not
to risk an action, unless with almost a certainty of
success. His Excellency marched at day-break on
the 5th, from Hollymount, through Clare to
Ballyhaunis, and the Yeomanry Corps of Mayo
were ordered to return to their former stations in
that county.

During the march to Ballyhaunis, and very near
that place, Lord Cornwallis received information
from Lieutenant-General Lake, and from his own
patroles, that the enemy was marching, with the
utmost expedition, towards Sligo, and had passed
Tubber curry, where he had been slightly engaged
with the Yeomanry of the place. His Excellency
upon this, determined to reinforce Lieutenant-
General Lake's corps, and Major-General Moore
accordingly marched very early in the morning of
the 6th, with the 100th regiment, and the two
flank battalions, in the direction of Tubber-curry.
His Excellency, with the remainder of the corps
proposed marching upon Carrick, there to pass the
Shannon, and to proceed up the Eastern Bank of
that river; regulating his subsequent movements
according to those of the enemy. Orders were
sent to the garrison of Sligo, not to wait the enemy's

my's attack in that open and defenceless town, but to retire to Ballyshannon or Enniskillen.

Reports were received at Ballyhaunis, that serious disturbances were taking place in the counties of Westmeath and Longford; that the people were rising in the neighbourhood of Ballimore, Granard, Rathown, the Islands of Rathaspick, Mullingar, Kilbeggan, &c. and had proceeded to acts of rebellion. Major General Trench had, in consequence, detached from the Garrison of Athlone to Ballimore, &c. and had ordered Brigadier General Dunne to reinforce Mullingar from Tullamore. Major General Nugent had also ordered a detachment of the Argyll Fencibles, from Belturbet and Cavan, to Granard, which, however, returned, upon receiving information that the rebels assembled in its neighbourhood, had been defeated, with great slaughter, by the Yeomanry Corps under Lord Longford and Captain Cottingham.

In consequence of these events, and the apprehensions which appeared to be entertained in every part of the Counties of Longford and Westmeath, that the rebellion was spreading, and was likely soon to become formidable, his Excellency thought proper to order the Brigade of Guards from Birr to Kilbeggan, where they would also be at hand, should it be found necessary to send troops

to

to Dublin, where fome difpofition to difturbance had been manifefted; boats were accordingly ordered to be held in readinefs at Phillip's Town, for their conveyance by Canal.

On the 6th the corps under Lord Cornwallis's command, proceeded to French Park, where His Excellency received reports from Major General Nugent and Lieutenant General Lake, of an unfuccefsful attack, which had, on the preceding day, been made by Colonel Vereker, with a part of the Garrifon of Sligo, upon the enemy, who had proceeded in the direction of Sligo, and had halted at Colooney.

Colonel Vereker having received information that a detachment of the enemy was at Colooney, and intended from thence to move round by Drumahair, to fupport the attack to be made upon Sligo, by Ballifadore, and under the impreffion that the main body of the enemy had remained in Caftlebar, marched from Sligo with about 270 men of the Limerick City Militia, 30 of the Twen-fourth Dragoons, and 2 curricle guns, which, from the information he had received, he thought a force equal to the attack of the enemy. The engagement took place about a quarter of a mile to the northward of Colooney, and was warmly maintained for the fpace of an hour, when the

D French,

French, by their great superiority of numbers, were enabled to out-flank, and to force Colonel Vereker's right, and obliged him to retreat. The officers and men of the Limerick City Regiment, behaved most gallantly in the action, and suffered considerably. Captain Cripps, their adjutant, was killed; Colonel Vereker, the Lieutenant Colonel, the Major, and two Subalterns were wounded; two Captains and two Subalterns taken prisoners. Had the enemy been opposed with equal firmness by some of the corps at Castlebar, he would probably never have reached Colooney.

Colonel Vereker retreated to Sligo, which he evacuated, retiring to Ballyshannon, upon finding that the enemy had on the night of the 5th, marched round by Drumahair and Ballitogher, apparently on his route to Sligo.

M. General Nugent, upon the receipt of Colonel Vereker's report, sent Brigadier General Champagné to Ballyshannon, with orders to attend to the defences of that place and of Beleck. The Queen's County Regiment was destined to reinforce these posts if required, and the Argyll Regiment was ordered from Belturbet to Enniskillen.

Major General Moore's corps arrived and encamped near Tobbercurry, on the evening of the
6th,

6th, having marched 19 Irish miles without halting. Lieutenant General Lake, on the morning of the same day, arrived at Colooney, from which place the enemy had marched the preceding night to Drumahair. Lieutenant General Lake immediately proceeded to Ballentogher, having sent forward Lieutenant Colonel Craufurd with a strong patrole towards Drumahair.

On the march from Colooney he found three six-pounders and one tumbril (British) which the enemy had difmounted and thrown into the ditch by the road fide; and Lieutenant Colonel Craufurd reported, that the enemy had marched at 11 o'clock A. M. on the 6th, from Drumahair to Manor Hamilton, having previoufly thrown five guns and one tumbril (British) over the bridge at the former place.

Lieutenant General Lake proceeded to Drumahair, and having received a further report that the enemy had fuddenly turned to the right at Drumkiern, he fent orders to Colonel Vereker to march back to Sligo, with the garrifon and the yeomanry that were retiring to Ballyfhannon, their abfence having created much uneafinefs in the country.

Lord Cornwallis judging from the enemy's

movements

movements, that it was his intention to proceed to Boyle, or Carrick on Shannon, haftened the march of his troops from French Park to the latter place, which they reached on the 7th, after a moft rapid march.

Major General Moore, who was at Tobbercurry, and who by the fudden turn the enemy had taken, was thrown one day's march in the rear of Lieutenant General Lake's corps, was directed to be prepared in the event of the enemy's movement to Boyle.

The Brigade of Guards was ordered from Kilbeggan to Mullingar, and to move on to the Southward a little in advance of Lord Cornwallis's corps.

Lieutenant Colonel Craufurd, who had never loft fight of the enemy, came up clofe to their rear guard on the 7th, between Drumfhambo and Ballinamore, killed a few, and caufed the infantry to form, which being pofted in ditches he could not attack. Lieutenant General Lake had proceeded with the utmoft expedition with the remainder of his corps, and encamped about two miles in front of Drumfhambo, on the fame day.

From henceforth, the movements of the different corps

corps are so clearly and so circumstantially stated in Lord Cornwallis's public letter of the 9th September, to the Duke of Portland, that it is perfectly unnecessary to enter into any further details, and I have, therefore, annexed a copy of it.

COPY *of the* LORD LIEUTENANT's LETTER *to the* DUKE *of* PORTLAND.

St. John's Town, County of Longford,
9th Sept. 1798.

" My Lord,

" When I wrote to Your Grace on the 5th, I had every reason to believe, from the enemy's movement to Drumehair, that it was their intention to march to the North, and it was natural to suppose, that they might hope that a French force would get into some of the bays in that part of the country, without a succour of which kind every point of direction for their march seemed equally desperate. I received, however, very early in the morning of the 7th, accounts from General Lake, that they had turned to their right at Drumkeirn, and that he had reason to believe that it was their intention to go to Boyle or Carrick on Shannon ; in consequence of which, I hastened the march of the troops under my immediate command, in order to arrive before the enemy at Carrick, and directed Major General Moore, who was at Tobbercurry, to be prepared in the event

D 3   of

of the enemy's movement to Boyle. On my arrival at
Carrick I found that the enemy had paffed the
Shannon at Balintra, where they had attempted to
deſtroy the bridge, but General Lake followed
them ſo cloſely, that they were not able to effect it.
Under theſe circumſtances, I felt pretty confident,
that one more march would bring this diſagreeable
warfare to a concluſion ; and having obtained ſatis-
factory information that the enemy had halted for
the night at Cloon ;. I marched, with the troops at
Carrick, at ten o'clock, on the night of the 7th, to
Mohill, and directed General Lake to proceed at
the ſame time to Cloon, which is about three miles
from Mohill, by which movement I ſhould be able
to join with General Lake in the attack of the
enemy, if they ſhould remain at Cloon, or to intercept their retreat, if they ſhould, as it was moſt pro-
bable, retire on the approach of our army. On my
arrival at Mohill, ſoon after day-break, I found that
the enemy had begun to move towards Granard ;
I therefore proceeded, with all poſſible expedition,
to this place, through which I was aſſured, on account of a broken bridge, that the enemy muſt paſs
in their way to Granard, and directed General
Lake to attack the enemy's rear, and impede their
march as much as poſſible, without bringing the
whole of his corps into action. Lieutenant General Lake performed this ſervice with his uſual attention and ability, and the encloſed letter which I
have

have juſt received from him, will explain the circumſtances which produced an immediate ſur-
render of the enemy's army. * The copy of my
orders which I encloſe will ſhow how much reaſon
I have to be ſatisfied with the exertions of the
troops, and I requeſt that your Grace will be
pleaſed to inform his Majeſty, that I have received
the greateſt aſſiſtance from the General and Staff
who have ſerved with the army.

I have, &c.

(Signed)   CORNWALLIS,

His Grace
The Duke of Portland, &c.

 Lieutenant General Lake, in the report alluded
to in his Excellency's letter, ſtates, that after four
days and nights moſt ſevere marching, his column
arrived at Cloon about ſeven o'clock on the morning of the 8th, when, after having received directions from Lord Cornwallis to follow the enemy
on the ſame line, while his Excellency moved by
the lower road to intercept him, he advanced, having previouſly detached the Monaghan Light Com-

* Note 5.

pany,

pany, mounted behind dragoons, to harrafs the enemy's rear. Lieutenant Colonel Craufurd, on coming up with the French rear guard, fummoned them to furrender, but as they did not attend to his fummons, he attacked them, upon which upwards of 200 French infantry threw down their arms. Under the idea that the remainder of the corps would do the fame, Captain Packenham, Lieutenant General of the Ordnance, and Major General Cradock, Quartermafter General, rode up to them. The enemy, however, inftantly commenced a fire of cannon and mufquetry, from which General Cradock received a wound in the arm. Lieutenant General Lake then ordered the 3d battalion of light infantry, under the command of Lieutenant Colonel Innis, of the 64th regiment, fupported by part of the Armagh Regiment of Militia, to commence the attack upon the enemy's pofition. The action lafted upwards of half an hour, when the remainder of the column making its appearance, the French furrendered at difcretion. The rebels (whofe force, notwithftanding the great reduction which had taken place in it from defertion, during the march, ftill amounted to about 1500,) difperfed, but numbers of them were killed on the field and in their flight. Mr. Blake was taken prifoner, and afterwards executed in purfuance of the fentence of a general court martial.

Lieutenant

Lieutenant General Lake, in his report, speaks in high terms of the conduct of the officers and men under his command, and particularly mentions Lieutenant Colonel Craufurd, of whose zeal, spirit, and abilities, too much cannot indeed be said; and whose exertions were admirably seconded by the detachment of Hompefch Dragoons, under the command of Captain O'Toole, of that corps. The following is the return of the loss suffered by the King's troops at Ballinamuck:

Killed.—Officers none; privates 3; horses 11.
Wounded.—Officer 1; privates 12; horse 1.
Missing.—Privates 3; horses 8.

It may be naturally supposed, that in a country where no magazines were established, considerable and unavoidable difficulties must have occurred in supplying the troops which had been suddenly marched into it, and whose movements in every direction were entirely unexpected. The manner in which the troops were nevertheless supplied, and which at no time afforded cause for complaint, speaks sufficiently in praise of the abilities and the exertions of Colonel Handfield, the Commiffary General.

Having,

Having, I truſt, proved ſatisfactorily that no delay had taken place previous to the arrival of Lord Cornwallis's corps at Hollymount, which was not indiſpenſably neceſſary from prudential motives, and of which the conſequences had undergone the moſt ſerious conſideration in all their effects, I cannot conclude this ſtatement without recommending to attention, the movements of the different corps from that period, for an explanation of which I muſt refer to the annexed map of the ſeat of operations.

To thoſe who have expatiated on the activity of the enemy, and the rapidity of his progreſs, it appears neceſſary to obſerve, that his precipitate march from Caſtlebar had given him a day's advance on both Lieutenant General Lake's and Lord Cornwallis's corps; that he moved without baggage, forcing a ſupply wherever he paſſed; and that ſo much was expedition his principal object, that he had even abandoned the greater part of his artillery on his route. Notwithſtanding which he was overtaken in one direction by Lieutenant General Lake's corps, and intercepted in another by Lord Cornwallis's; the exertions and activity of whoſe troops muſt therefore be admitted to have been ſuperior even to thoſe which have with ſome individuals been ſo much a ſubject of admiration.

No

No inconvenience refulted to the country from the continuance of the enemy at Caftlebar having been protracted for the fpace of three days, but the confequences would perhaps have proved fatal had the defperate effort which he made upon the approach of the King's troops, and which was evidently directed against the capital, been attempted before Lord Cornwallis had affembled fuch a force as enabled him to act with energy, and until the prefence and example of fome experienced troops had given confidence to his corps, in great meafure compofed of regiments brave and zealous indeed, but unexperienced. It was alfo effentially neceffary for his Excellency to reinforce the corps on his right, with a view to impede the enemy's movements in that quarter.

Lord Cornwallis's march to Carrick on Shannon, was equally calculated to counteract the enemy's operations, had he penetrated into the North, as it was to oppofe his progrefs to the capital, but the latter was a confideration of fuch infinite importance, that his Excellency was further induced to direct the march of the brigade of Guards to Mullingár and Kilbeggan, where its prefence muft ultimately have defeated the enemy's project, had he by the rapidity of his march fucceeded in efcaping the two corps immediately in purfuit of him, whilft it contributed effentially to
the

the reftoration of order in the counties of Weftmeath and Kildare, and to its prefervation in Dublin
and the neighbourhood.

The circumftances which had required fuch
movements and precautions, cannot again occur,
fhould even a force of the enemy, far fuperior to
that under General Humbert, effect a landing upon
the Irifh coaft. The difpofition of the troops
which was ordered, although not executed, when
General Humbert landed, having fince taken place,
and the zeal and loyalty of the Englifh militia,
having enabled Government to fend fuch reinforcements to Ireland as, combined with the laudable
exertions and the active fpirit which have upon fo
many trying occafions been manifefted by the
yeomanry of Ireland, muft enfure the poffibility of
providing without delay, againft foreign attempts,
and of fuppreffing internal rifings.

APPENDIX.

NOTE I.

LIBERTY, EQUALITY, FRATERNITY, UNION!

IRISHMEN,

YOU have not forgot Bantry Bay—you know what efforts France has made to affift you. Her affections for you, her defire for avenging your wrongs, and affuring your independance, can never be impaired.

After feveral unfuccefsful attempts, behold Frenchmen arrived amongft you.

They come to fupport your courage, to fhare your dangers, to join their arms, and to mix their blood with yours in the facred caufe of liberty. They are the forerunners of other Frenchmen, whom you fhall foon infold in your arms.

Brave

Brave IRISHMEN, our caufe is common; like you, we abhor the avaricious and blood-thirfty policy of an oppreffive government; like you, we hold as indefeafible the right of all nations to liberty; like you, we are perfuaded that the peace of the world fhall ever be troubled, as long as the Britifh Miniftry is fuffered to make with impunity a traffic of the induftry, labour, and blood of the people.

But exclufive of the fame interefts which unite us, we have powerful motives, to love and defend you.

Have we not been the pretext of the cruelty exercifed againft you by the Cabinet of St. James's? The heartfelt intereft you have fhewn in the grand events of our revolution—Has it not been imputed to you as a crime? Are not tortures and death continually hanging over fuch of you as are barely fufpected of being our friends? Let us unite, then, and march to glory.

We fwear the moft inviolable refpect for your properties, your laws, and all your religious opinions. Be free; be mafters in your own country. We look for no other conqueft than that of your liberty—no other fuccefs than yours.

The

The moment of breaking your chains is arrived; our triumphant troops are now flying to the extremities of the earth, to tear up the roots of the wealth and tyranny of our enemies. That frightful Coloſſus is mouldering away in every part. Can there be any Iriſhman baſe enough to ſeparate himſelf at ſuch a happy conjuncture from the grand intereſts of his country? If ſuch there be, brave friends, let him be chaſed from the country he betrays, and let his property become the reward of thoſe generous men who know how to fight and die.

Iriſhmen, recollect the late defeats which your enemies have experienced from the French; recollect the Plains of Honſcoote, Toulon, Quiberon, and Oſtend; recollect America, free from the moment ſhe wiſhed to be ſo.

The conteſt between you and your oppreſſors cannot be long.

Union! Liberty! the Iriſh Republic!—ſuch is our ſhout. Let us march. Our hearts are devoted to you; our glory is in your happineſs.

NOTE

NOTE II.

ARMEE D'IRLANDE.

Au Quartier Général à Caſtlebar, le ouze Fructidor, an ſix de la République Françaiſe.

LE GENERAL COMMANDANT EN CHEF L'ARMEE D'IRLANDE AU DIRECTOIRE EXECUTIF.

JE vous dois, Citoyens Directeurs, le rapport de mes opérations depuis mon arriveé en Irlande.

Le 4me Fructidor, l'armée a été nommeé l'armée d'Irlande, dèſque j'ai apperçu les attèrages de Broadhaven. Les vents étant contraires il n'a pas été poſſible d'approcher terre de ce jour.

Le 5me, la diviſion de frégates aprés avoir lutté pendant douze heures contre les vents et les courants a mouillé dans la baye de Killala, vers les trois heures de l'apres midi. Comme le Pavillon Anglais était arborê nous avons eu la viſite de pluſieurs perſonnes de marque et de quelques officiers Anglais,

Anglais, dont l'étonnement à notre vue ne peut se dépeindre. A quatre heures le débarquement à été ordonné. L'Adjutant Général Sarrazin a débarqué le premier à la tète des grenadiers; je lui ai donné l'ordre de marcher fur Killala dont il s'éft emparé à la bayonette : Je l'ai nommé General de Brigade fur ie champ de bataille. L'ennemi a été dérouté completement;—de ce pofte gardé par deux cents hommes, une vingtaine fe font fauvés à travers les murailles, les autres ont été pris ou tués. Prefque tous les prifonniers ont demandé à fervir avec nous, je le leur ai accordé avec plaifir. Le débarquement était totalement effectué vers les dix heures du foir.

Le 6me, le Général Sarrazin a été reconnaitre *Ballina*, il n'y a eû qu'une légere efcarmouche, la cavalerie ennemie s'etant retirée au grand galop pendant plus de deux lieues.

Le 7me, j'ai marché avec l'armée fur Ballina. Le Général Sarrazin a la tête des grenadiers et d'un bataillon de ligne a culbuté tout ce qui s'eft oppofé à fon paffage. L'Adjutant Général Fontaine a été chargé de tourner l'ennemi, fon attaque a trés bien reuffi, et il a fait plufieurs prifonniers. J'ai pourfuivi pendant longtems la cavalerie avec le brave troifieme regiment de chaffeurs à cheval.

E   Le

Le 8me, l'armeé Françaife a été jointe par un corps d'Irlandais Unis, qui ont été armés et habillés fur le champ ; vers les trois heures du foir je me fuis porté fur Rappa, j'ai gardé cette pafible jufqu'à deux heures après minuit.

Le 9me, l'armeé a marché fur Ballina, où elle a pris pofition, elle eu eft partie à trois heures de l'aprés midi. Apres une marche de quinze heures, je fuis arrivé le 10me, à 6 heures du matin, fur les hauteurs en arriere de Caftlebar, j'ai reconnu la pofition de l'ennemi qui etait tres forte, j'ai ordonné au Général Sarrazin de commencer l'attaque. Les Tirailleurs de l'ennemi ont été repouffés vivement. Le Chef de Bataillon Dufour les a chaffé jufqu'au pied de la pofition de l'armeé ennemie. Les grenadiers fe font portés au pas de charge fur la ligne de bataille, l'infanterie de ligne les a fuivi, le déployment des colonnes s'eft opéré fous le feu de douze pieces de canon. Le Général Sarrazin a fait attaquer la gauche de l'ennemi, par un bataillon de ligne, qui a été obligé de fe réplier effuyant le feu de plus de deux mille hommes. Le Général Sarrazin vole a fon fecours à la tête des grenadiers et repouffe l'ennemi. Les Anglais font pendant une demi heure un feu terrible de moufqueterie. Le Général Sarrazin défend qu'on ripofte. Notre contenance fière deconcerte le Général Anglais. Defque l'armeé eft toute arriveé

j'ordonne

j'ordonne l'attaque générale. Le Général Sarrazin à la tête des grenadiers culbute la droite de
l'ennemi et s'empare de trois pieces de canon, le
Chef de Bataillon Ardouin force la gauche de l'ennemi à replier dans Caftlebar. L'ennemi con-
centré dans la ville et foutenu par fon artillerie fait
un feu terrible. Le troifieme regiment de chaffeurs effectue une charge dans la grande rue de
Caftlebar, et force l'ennemi à paffer de l'autre côté
du pont. Aprés plufieures charges trés meurtri-
eres de cavalerie et d'infanterie dirigees par le
Général Sarrazin et l'Adjutant Général Fontaine,
l'ennemi a été chaffé de toutes fes pofitions, et
pourfuivi encore pendant deux lieues.

L'ennemi a perdu dix huit cents hommes dont
fix cents tués ou bleffés et douze cents prifonniers,
dix pieces de canon, cinq drapeaux, douze cent
fufils, et prefque tous les equipages. Le drapeau
de la cavalerie ennemie a été enlevé dans une
charge par le Général Sarrazin, que j'ai nommé
Général de Divifion fur le champ de bataille.
J'ai auffi nommé pendant l'action l'Adjutant Général Fontaine, Général de Brigade, les Chefs de
Bataillon Azemare, Ardouin et Dufour, Chefs de
Brigade, le Capitaine Durival Chef d'Efcadron, et
les Capitaines Touffaint, Zilberman, Ranon, Huette,
Babiu, et Rutz, Chefs de Bataillon. Je vous prie
Citoyens Directeurs, de confirmer ces nominations

et

et de faire expedier les brevets le plutot poffible cela produira un très bon effet.

. Officiers et foldats tous ont fait des prodiges— Nous avons à regretter d'excellents officiers, et de bien braves foldats. Je vous enverrais bientôt d'autres détails, il me fuffit de vous dire que l'armeé ennemie forte de 5 à 6 mille hommes, dont fix cent de cavalerie a été totalement deroutée.

Salut et Refpeét.

NOTE

NOTE II. (Tranſlation.)

———

ARMY OF IRELAND.

*Head Quarters at Caſtlebar, 11th Fructi-
dor, 6th Year of the French Republic.*

THE GENERAL COMMANDING IN CHIEF THE
ARMY OF IRELAND, TO THE EXECUTIVE
DIRECTORY.

I AM to report to you, Citizens Directors, what
have been my operations in Iréland.

On the 4th Fructidor, as ſoon as I got within
ſight of Broadhaven, the army received the ap-
pellation of Army of Ireland. The wind being
unfavourable, we could not make the land on that
day.

On the 5th, the diviſion of frigates, after beat-
ing againſt wind and tide during 12 hours, an-
chored in the Bay of Killala about three o'clock
P. M. In conſequence of our having hoiſted the

Engliſh

Englifh flag, many perfons of note, and fome English officers, came on board;—it is impoffible to defcribe their aftonifhment at the fight of us.— At four, orders were given to difembark. The Adjutant General Sarazin landed firft, at the head of the grenadiers. I ordered him to march to Killala, which he carried with the bayonet. I appointed him General of Brigade on the field of battle. The enemy was compleatly defeated. Of 200 men who defended the poft, about 20 only efcaped over the walls—the reft were taken or killed. Almoft all the prifoners begged to be permitted to ferve with us, and I readily confented to their requeft. The difembarkation was compleated towards 10 o'clock P. M.

On the 6th, General Sarrazin reconnoitred Ballina ; a flight fkirmifh only took place, the enemy's cavalry having retired in full gallop the fpace of two leagues.

On the 7th, I marched with the army againft Ballina. General Sarazin, at the head of the grenadiers and of one battalion of the line, difperfed every thing that oppofed his paffage. The Adjutant General Fontaine was directed to turn the enemy's flank. This attack fucceeded, and he took feveral prifoners. I purfued the cavalry during

during a confiderable time, with the brave 3d
regiment of Chaffeurs à Cheval.

On the 8th, the French army was joined by a
corps of United Irifhmen, who were armed and
clothed on the fpot. Towards three o'clock P. M.
I moved forward to Rappa, and remained in that
direction until two o'clock A. M.

On the 9th, the army advanced to Ballina, where
it took poft, but marched from it at three o'clock
P. M.—After a march of 15 hours, I arrived on
the 10th, at fix o'clock in the morning, on the
heights in the rear of Caftlebar. Having ex-
amined the enemy's pofition, which was very
ftrong, I ordered General Sarrazin to commence
the attack. The enemy's fkirmifhers were rapidly
driven in, and were purfued as far as the foot of
the enemy's pofition. The grenadiers charged
their line of battle, and were fupported by the infantry of the line. The columns deployed under
the fire of 12 pieces of cannon. General Sarrazin
ordered the enemy's left to be attacked by a battalion of the line, which was obliged to give way,
having received the fire of upwards of 2000 men.
General Sarrazin flew to its fupport at the head of
the grenadiers, and repulfed the enemy. The
Englifh, during half an hour, kept up a tremendous
fire of mufquetry, to which General Sarrazin for-

E 4   bid

bid repofting. Our determined countenance dif-
concerted the Englifh General, and as foon as the
whole of the army had come up, I ordered a general
attack to be made. General Sarrazin drove in
the enemy's right, and took three pieces of cannon.
The Chief of Battalion, Ardouin, obliged his left to
retire to Caftlebar.

The enemy having concentrated his force in
Caftlebar, and protected by his artillery kept up a
terrible fire—but by a fuccefsful charge of the 3d
regiment of Chaffeurs à Cheval, made through the
main ftreet of Caftlebar, he was forced to retire
acrofs the bridge. After feveral very deftructive
charges, both of cavalry and infantry, directed by
General Sarrazin and Adjutant General Fontaine, the enemy was driven from all his pofitions,
and purfued for the fpace of two leagues.

The enemy's lofs amounts to 1800 men (of
which 600 killed or wounded, and 1200 prifoners),
10 pieces of cannon, 5 ftand of colours, 1200 firelocks, and almoft all his baggage. The ftandard
of his cavalry was taken in a charge by General
Sarrazin, whom I named General of Divifion on
the field of battle. I alfo, during the action, appointed the Adjutant General Fontaine, General of
Brigade, and the Chiefs of Battalion Azemare,
Ardouin, and Dufour, Chiefs of Brigade. I further

ther named Captain Durival a Commander of Squa-
-dron, and Captains Touffaint, Zilberman, Ranou,
Huette, Babiu, and Rutz, Chiefs of Battalion.
I beg, Citizens Directors, that you will be pleased
to confirm thefe promotions, and that you will fend
the commiffions as foon as poffible, as it will be
productive of very good effects.

Officers and foldiers have fhewn prodigies of
valour. We have to regret the lofs of fome excellent officers and very brave foldiers. I fhall very
fhortly forward to you further details; at prefent I
will only add, that the enemy's army, confifting of
between 5 and 6000 men, of which 600 cavalry,
has been completely difperfed.

Health and Refpect.

(Signed) HUMBERT.

NOTE

NOTE III.

ARMEE D'IRLANDE.

Au Quartier Général à Caftlebar le 11me Fructidor, an 6me de la République Française.

LE GENERAL COMMANDANT EN CHEF L'ARMEE D'IRLANDE, AU MINISTRE DE LA MARINE.

JE vous envoye, Citoyen Miniftre, copie de ma lettre au Directoire Exécutif. Elle vous prouvera que nous faifons tous nos efforts pour remplir les vues du gouvernment. J'ai fait plufieurs nominations d'après les actions et les talens militaires des individus qui en font l'objets. Je vous prie d'en foliciter la confirmation auprès du Directoire Exécutif.

Les Irlandais Unis m'ont rejoint au nombre de fix cents le 8me Fructidor, ils ont été armés et habillés fur le champ. Le 10 ils font venus jufque fur les hauteurs en arrière de Caftlebar. Ils ont pris la fuite au premier coup de canon, je m'y attendais

tendais et leur terreur panique n'a nullement derangé mes operations. La victoire de Castlebar a produite un bon effect. Je pense avoir sous trois jours un corps de deux à trois mille hommes du pays.

L'armeé Anglaise que j'ai battue hier est commandée par le Général Haughton. Son Quartier Général est à Tuam. Il se propose de réunir vingt cinq mille hommes pour prendre sa revanche. De mon côté je mets tout en usage pour le bien recevoir, et mème aller à son devant en raison des circonstances.

Nous sommes en possession de Killala, Ballina, Foxford, Castlebar, Newport, Ballinarobe, et Westport. Dès que le corps d'Irlandais Unis que je veux reunir à moi sera armé et habillé je marcherai à l'ennemi. Je me dirigerai vers Roscommon, où l'insurrection a de plus chauds partisans. Dès que l'armée Anglaise aura evacué la province de Connaught je passerai le Schanon et tacherai de faire joindre l'armee par les insurgés du nord. Cette réunion etant effectuée j'aurai assez de force pour marcher sur Dublin et livrer une bataille décisive.

Les Irlandais ont tatoné jusqu'a ce jour. Le Comté de Mayo n'a jamais été en insurrection, aussi

auſſi nos progrês ne ſont pas auſſi rapides qûils l'euſſent été par tout ailleurs. Comme il eſt poſſible que la poignée de Français ſuccombe ſous le nombre et que nos nouveaux ſoldats ſoyent effrayés par le bruit du canon comme à Caſtlebar je vous demande un bataillon et la 3me ½ brigade d'infanterie légére, un de la 10me ¼ brigade de ligne, cent ciquante hommes du 3me regiment de chaſſeurs à cheval et cent canoniers d'artillerie légere, quinze mille fuſils, et un million de cartouches. Avec le renfort que j'evalue à deux mille hommes, je crois pouvoir aſſurer qu'un mois après ſon arrivée l'Irlande ſera libre. La Flotte pourra mouiller dans la Bay de Tarboy par 53^q 55' de latitude du ſud de l'Iſle Mulete, le debarquement s'effeêtuera ſans obſtacle.

Je ne puis trop faire l'eloge du corps de troupes à mes ordres. Je recommende mes braves camrades à la reconnaiſſance nationale et à votre follicitude paternelle.

Salut et Reſpeêt.

(Signé)

HUMBERT.

NOTE

NOTE III. (Tranflation).

ARMY OF IRELAND.

Head Quarters, Caftlebar, 11th Fruƈtidor, 6th year of the French Republic.

THE GENERAL COMMANDING IN CHIEF THE ARMY OF IRELAND, TO THE MINISTER OF MARINE.

I TRANSMIT to you, Citizen Minifter, the copy of my letter to the Executive Direƈtory. You will perceive that no exertions are wanting on our part to fulfill the intentions of Government.

I have made feveral appointments, according to the aƈtions and to the military talents difplayed by thofe whom they regard, and I folicit your fupport in obtaining from the Executive Direƈtory, a confirmation of them.

About 600 United Irifh joined me on the 8th Fruƈtidor, and were immediately armed and clothed.

clothed. On the 10th they came forward to the heights in the rear of Caftlebar. The firft cannon fhot that was fired drove them off. I expected as much, and their panic in no way deranged my operations.

The victory of Caftlebar has produced excellent effects; and I hope within three days to have with me a corps of 2 or 3000 of the inhabitants.

The Englifh army, which I yefterday defeated, is commanded by General Houghton, whofe head quarters are now at Tuam. He intends to affemble 25,000 men to attack me; and on my fide I am doing my utmoft to be well prepared for his reception, and even to go and meet him fhould circumftances juftify fuch proceeding. We occupy Killala, Ballina, Foxford, Caftlebar, Newport, Ballinrobe, and Weftport. As foon as the corps of United Irifhmen, which I wifh to affemble, fhall be clothed, I fhall march againft the enemy in the direction of Rofcommon, where the partizans of infurrection are moft zealous. As foon as the Englifh army fhall have evacuated the Province of Connaught, I fhall pafs the Shannon, and fhall endeavour to make a junction with the infurgents in the North. When this fhall have been effected, I fhall be in a fufficient force to march to Dublin, and to fight a decifive action.

The

The Irish have until this day hung back. The county of Mayo has never been disturbed, and this must account for the slowness of our progress, which in other parts would have been very different.

As this handful of French may possibly be obliged to yield to numbers, and that the noise of cannon may again produce on our new soldiers the effect it had at Castlebar, I desire you will send me one battalion of the 3d half brigade of light infantry, one of the 10th half brigade of the line, 150 of the 3d regiment of chasseurs a cheval, and 100 men of the light artillery; 15,000 firelocks, and a million of cartridges.

I will venture to assert, that in the course of a month after the arrival of this reinforcement, which I estimate at 2000 men, Ireland will be free.

The fleet may anchor in the Bay of *Tarboy*, by 53, 55 latitude South of *L'Isle Muttette*, and the disembarkation will be effected without difficulty.

I cannot sufficiently praise the conduct of the troops under my command. I must recommend my brave comrades to the gratitude of the nation, and to your paternal care.

(Signed)　　HUMBERT.

NOTE

NOTE IV.

ARMEE D'IRLANDE.

LIBERTE, EGALITE.

Au Quartier Général à Caſtlebar, le 14me Fructidor, an 6me de la République Françaiſe, une et indiviſible.

LE Général Humbert, Commandant en Chef l'Armée d'Irlande, deſirant organiſer dans le plus bréf délai, un pouvoir adminiſtratif pour la province de Connaught, arrête ce qui ſuit :

1re. Le Gouvernement de la province de Connaught reſidera a Caſtlebar juſqu'à nouvel ordre.

2de.

2de. Ce Gouvernement fera compofé de douze membres, qui feront nommés par le Général en Chef de l'armée Françaife.

3me. Le Citoyen Jean Moore eft nommé Préfident du Gouvernement de la province de Connaûght. Il eft fpécialement chargé de la nomination et réunion des membres du gouvernement.

4me. Le Gouvernement s'occupera fur le champ d'organifer la milice de la Province de Connaught, et d'affurer les fubfiftances des armées Françaife et Irlandaife.

5me. Il fera organifé huit regiments d'infanterie chacun de douze cents hommes, et quatre regiments de cavalerie chacun de fix cents hommes.

6me. Le Gouvernement declarera rebelle et traitre à la patrie, tout ceux qui ayant reçu des habits ou des armes ne ne rejoindraient pas l'armeé dans les vingt quatres heures.

7me. Tout individu depuis feize ans jufqu'à quarante inclufivement eft requis au nom de la Republique Irlandaife de fe rendre de fuite au camp Français pour marcher en maffe contre l'ennemi commun le tiran de l'Irlande—l'Anglais; dont le de-

F   ftruction

ftruction peut feule affurer l'indépendance et le
bonheur de l'antique Hibernie.

(Signé)

Le General Commandant en Chef,

HUMBERT.

NOTE

NOTE IV. (Tranſlation).

ARMY OF IRELAND.

LIBERTY, EQUALITY.

Head Quarters at Caſtlebar, 14th *Fructidor,* 6th *year of the French Republic, one
and indiviſible.*

GENERAL Humbert, Commanding in Chief the
Army of Ireland, being deſirous of organizing,
with as little delay as poſſible, an adminiſtrative
power for the province of Connaught, directs as
follows:

1ſt. The ſeat of the government ſhall be at
Caſtlebar, until further orders.

2d.

2d. The Government ſhall be formed of 12 members, who ſhall be named by the Commander in Chief of the French army.

3d. Citizen John Moore is appointed Preſident of the Government of the province of Connaught, and is ſpecially entruſted with the nomination and the uniting of its members.

4th. The Government ſhall immediately attend to the organization of the militia of the province of Connaught, and to the ſupplies for the French and Iriſh armies.

5th. Eight regiments of infantry of 1200 men each, and four regiments of cavalry of 600 men each, ſhall be organized.

6th. The government ſhall declare all thoſe to be rebels and traitors, who having received arms, or cloathing, ſhall not within 24 hours rejoin the army.

7th. Every individual, from the age of 16 to 40 incluſive, is required in the name of the Iriſh Republic, inſtantly to repair to the French camp, in order to march in maſs againſt the common enemy, the tyrant of Ireland—the Engliſh; whoſe deſtruction

ſtruction alone can inſure the independence and the welfare of antient Hibernia.

(Signed)

The General Commanding in Chief,

HUMBERT.

NOTE

NOTE V.

GENERAL ORDERS.

Head Quarters, near St. John's Town,
9th September, 1798.

LORD Cornwallis cannot too much applaud the zeal and fpirit which has been manifefted by the army, from the commencement of the operations againft the invading enemy, until the furrender of the French forces.

The perfeverance with which the foldiers fupported the extraordinary marches which were neceffary to ftop the progrefs of the very active enemy, does them the greateft credit; and Lord Cornwallis heartily congratulates them on the happy iffue of their meritorious exertions.

The corps of yeomanry, in the whole country through which the army has paffed, have rendered

the

the greateft fervices, and are peculiarly entitled to the acknowledgments of the Lord Lieutenant, for their not having tarnifhed that courage and loyalty which they difplayed in the caufe of their King and country, by any acts of wanton cruelty towards their deluded fellow fubjects.

FINIS.

Lightning Source UK Ltd.
Milton Keynes UK
UKHW051515130819
347804UK00011B/69/P